MW00967036

UNBROKEN

A COLLECTION OF STORIES

J.S. ROSEN

Text © 2021 by J.S. Rosen

All rights reserved. No part of this publication may be reproduced, stored, or transmitted in any form or by any means, electronic, mechanical, photocopying, recording, scanning, or otherwise without written permission from the publisher. It is illegal to copy this book, post it to a website, or distribute it by any other means without permission.

ISBN: 978-1-0880-7516-6

Table of Contents

Foreword

Losing a grandparent. Going to college. Getting divorced.

It seems that, no matter what journey we find ourselves on, family has a way of influencing our lives. In this brief collection of stories, I hope to highlight some of the many ways in which family can shape us, or even break us. Perhaps these stories will cause you to think of your own fondest memories. Perhaps you'll recall the ones you never thought you'd dig up again.

Either way, I hope your resilience and your journey remain unbroken. Happy trails.

- J.S. Rosen

Unbroken

I'm only here tonight because baseball is not America's pastime. It's the kind of game that your parents send you to play when you're five, and the one you're screaming at on television from your couch with you're fifty. Tonight, however, it's one of those games where the family in front of you stands every ten minutes to bring their daughter to the restroom or grab a snack, and the guy to your right becomes further inebriated each time the Pirates bat in a run. Soon enough, he doesn't know which team he's cheering for.

I look to my left and notice my fiancé Cory is back on his tablet, answering work emails. Cory hates baseball—he thinks it's drawn out, boring, and that I'm crazy to go to as many games as I do. I've been to 498 in my lifetime; Cory hates that, too, and that's why I love him.

I don't try to distract him from work—he could not care less if Anthony Rizzo hit a foul ball onto the empty seat beside him. It's a chilly night at Wrigley Field, but I have on my old denim shorts designated specifically for baseball games. My brown hair is pulled back into a messy ponytail, and my makeup is just starting to fade from the crazy day at a job I'm obligated to say I enjoy.

Rizzo hits a fly ball into right field, opposite from where we sit, and the man on my right cheers both before and after the outfielder makes the catch. The booing of the Cubs fans rains down on us, and I simply crack a smile.

"These fuckin' calls, man," my right-hand neighbor slurs out. I make the mistake of catching his eye. "You a Cubs fan?" he asks.

I evaluate the man a bit more, since he's directly addressing me. He has blond hair with small speckles of gray, but he doesn't look much older than me, now that I think of it. There is an open seat between us, but I start to feel as though my bubble is close to rupturing. The bubble that houses Cory and me.

I shake my head. "Just a baseball fan."

The remark seems to throw the man off. It's meant to. "A baseball fan?"

I give him a quick nod and then return my attention to the game. "That's right."

"You a transplant, then?"

"Nope, born and raised in Chicago."

He contemplates my answer for a moment, and then extends his hand. "I'm Keith."

I respond with my name. "Maggie." Keith nods at Cory, who is still too absorbed in his email to notice our exchange. "What about him? He a homegrown hero, as well?"

I chuckle. "He's from New Orleans."

Keith nods and then mutters under his breath, "*Fuckin' transplants!*"

After a short time he distracts himself with another beer, and I focus my gaze on Andrew McCutchen, who's up to bat for Pittsburgh.

"Two-two pitch, and McCutchen pops it up into center field. Fowler is there to make the catch!" the announcer yells through the portable radio that I like to carry.

Keith boos.

* * *

I was eleven years old when my father placed a red, blue, and white cap on my head and told me I was going to be a baseball fan. Wrigley Field was just a drive away, he'd said, taking my hand and leading me to the car, where my mother waited. My family had never shown an interest in the sport before; we lived in the suburbs of Chicago—Northbrook to be exact—but any talk of the Cubs amongst relatives resulted in either mild cursing or complete apathy.

Since Corey Patterson's homerun during the second inning of my very first game, I had done nothing but sulk. The air was warm, and the crowd's enthusiasm attempted to envelop me like the ballpark cotton candy that was stuck to everything; this included the three-year-old's hair in front of us. A vendor had passed by three times now, trying to coax us into purchasing just one little swirl of pink and blue. "A bite-sized candy for a bite-sized girl," he'd said to me on Round Two.

But I, Maggie Duschene, was not a bite-sized girl. I also didn't want to be here tonight. In just a total of two months, my father had been laid off, Mom was slowly becoming obsessed with our bills, and she had developed a heightened interest in the amount of alcohol Dad imbibed each week. On top of all that, we were now going to like baseball. There was something to be said for ignoring a facet of life until the moment you most desperately needed it.

In the eyes of my parents, baseball was going to save my family. It was going to become the glue that kept us together. Luckily, I knew better, and I was simply counting the days.

I learned my first lesson about the Cubs during the bottom of the third inning. Derek Lee was up to bat and Dad sat back, placing an arm around my shoulder.

"You know the Cubs haven't won a World Series since 1908?" he asked.

I eyed him sideways. Perhaps we shouldn't

discuss such things in front of actual fans.

"It's true," he said, smiling. "Been just about a century since they were the champs."

The lessons and tidbits continued. Every few minutes, Dad pointed to something on the scoreboard across the field from us, explaining what a number meant, or a symbol. By the fourth inning, I had learned that an *error* occurred when a play that should have been made wasn't. By the top of the fifth, I understood that the Cubs were part of something called the National League, and within that, the Central Division. By the Seventh Inning Stretch, I was informed that we would be returning again tomorrow night.

As it turned out, season tickets to the Cubs were the pity gift of former coworkers when you were laid off. More facts.

The summer progressed. My father made it a routine to rattle off extra information he thought I needed, and I decided to humor him. I pictured him scouring the Internet, trying to understand how baseball worked. How it evolved, how it breathed, grew, triumphed, and failed. I wondered how much further he would go—how much energy it would take to keep up the charade that baseball could fix everything.

* * *

Cory nudges me. "What the hell is an RBI?" he asks. "Everyone around us keeps saying it."

I'm a little surprised by the question, but then again, Cory likes knowing things. He's an analyst at a bank. It must upset him to some extent, trying to understand a term that everyone around him seems to know.

"It stands for *Runs Batted In*," I tell him, then I smirk. "I'll let you figure out the rest."

He rolls his eyes and shoots me a grin in return. "Thanks, but I'll pass on the homework."

Homework was never his thing anyway, not even at Northwestern, where we met.

I was seventeen when I received my acceptance to the university—eighteen when I enrolled on a full ride. Mom was glad she could take what little tuition money she had managed to save up and put it toward our living expenses. We had long moved out of Northbrook.

In my first class, we were asked to say something interesting about ourselves. Most students introduced themselves and then talked about their three-legged pets, or their most recent volunteer trips to places like Honduras. When the circle got to me, however, I kept it simple. "I'm Maggie Duschene," I began, "and I've been to 457 baseball games in my life."

Most of the games following "the year of the season tickets" were courtesy of my childhood friends and their parents, but I didn't add that information. The classroom fell silent, and with each passing moment, I anticipated a response. Finally, the boy sitting across from me whispered, loud enough for the class to hear, "Not the fucking *Cubs*, right?"

The class laughed, and I joined in. The boy who had broken the ice for me was Cory, and by the end of the year I thought I was in love with him. By the end of second year, I knew I was.

Someone a few rows down from us snaps their

fingers and, within seconds, my mind stops wandering from the game at hand. I crane my neck, attempting to locate the source of the sound. Before I can, though, Cory shuts his tablet and takes my hand in his. "What inning is it?" he asks. But it's not out of interest.

"Just started the fifth," I reply. "Not yet."

He nods, understanding that we'll leave during the top of the sixth. We always do.

* * *

Pretending to enjoy the games with my parents became a talent of mine. Dad made it a habit to use the restroom in the sixth inning, when he claimed there "wasn't much to see," and I was always left pondering how he could know that for sure. I'd sit with my mother for another half-inning, maintaining my "enjoyment face," but also equally bored and unable to keep my eyes focused. The game dragged on and, even as I slowly became familiar with the names of the players—Walker, Martinez, Lee—I started wondering what they would do with their lives if they weren't part of the sport. If they didn't travel several months out of the year. Dad returned from the restrooms, but this time, he had no new facts to share.

One evening at Wrigley Field in late July, Mom flagged down the cotton candy vendor, a gesture that surprised even me. Dad had ordered a beer as soon as the top of the batting lineup got his first strikeout. Perhaps she was trying to teach him a lesson on frugality.

"You don't need that, hun," she had said to him as the vendor popped open the bottle and handed it over.

"I don't *need* to need it," he replied, winking at me. "Some things are just for enjoyment."

Now Mom held out the large pink and blue swirl-on-a-stick, as though she expected me to take it. I did, and a twang of guilt preceded every sticky bite that I took. Dad didn't seem to mind. Maybe Mom should have rethought her tactics.

"Ice cold beer! Get yer ice cold beer!" another vendor shouted as he passed our seats.

Luckily, Dad hadn't finished his first one.

A boy, maybe a few years older than me, sat a few rows down from us and attempted to flag the drink vendor over. He had blond hair, almost platinum in the stadium lights. He caught my eye and winked. I could see the sweat dripping through the vendor's blue shirt as he approached him, and I wondered who would ever want to do that job. The vendor shook his head at the blond boy, smiling as he made his way past him. But then he paused, doubled back, and tossed a bag of peanuts into the boy's lap. He laughed to himself before continuing on his way through the rows. The boy tore open the little bag of salty peanuts and eyed me again. But before he took his first bite, he nudged the man next to him—his father, presumably—and poured a small bit into his palm. The two enjoyed the treat for the rest of the inning.

In the bottom of the ninth, the Cubs lost 9–3, and we headed to the parking lot. The traffic was terrible, and we didn't get home until almost an hour later. When Mom tucked me in that night, she asked me how it felt to be a baseball fan, and I replied that I had no idea. She chuckled, kissed me on the forehead, and shut the light off.

* * *

Keith wants to talk about baseball being America's pastime.

He starts by discussing how his father always played catch with him as a kid. Then how his father walked out on his family and Keith became an alcoholic as a result of his deprived childhood. "Luckily," he says to me, "I've grown out of that habit." He takes another swig of his beer. "Can stop any time I want to. Like shutting off a light switch."

I nod politely and try to get Cory to engage me in conversation. He's back on his tablet, but I swear I almost see a smile tugging at his lips.

"You ever play ball? Softball, maybe?"

Keith's sexist comment would normally upset me, but at this point, I just want to enjoy the last inning we'll be here in peace. "No," I reply. "My parents never showed an interest in the game. Then my dad left us right here, at Wrigley Field, and after that he never showed an interest in anything." I smile sweetly, leaving Keith dumbfounded and finally unable to form words.

A vendor shouts for the patrons around us to buy more beer, and I expect Keith to flag him down, but he doesn't. He just stares into his nearly empty drink—still silent, still dumbfounded. I suppose I dropped the bomb when I shouldn't have. But, I have no regrets about that.

* * *

The summer moved into August, and our attendance at games had long become routine. On a particularly warm night while we were playing our age-old rival, the St. Louis Cardinals, I asked Dad why people kept coming to games, even though the Cubs had a less than desirable record.

"Well, you see," he began, reaching down to grab a bag that sat at his feet. "That's the beauty of it—things can turn around, just like that." He snapped his fingers and I jumped. Someone who was nearly deaf could hear Dad snap his fingers from a mile away.

"Is that why we keep coming?" I asked pointedly. "Because you think we'll finally win?"

Dad ran his fingers through my hair, tucking a lock behind my ear. "We've won lots of games!" he assured me. He didn't understand my question.

Dad had run off during his sixth inning restroom break and come back with the bag he now held in his arms. He grinned at me, opened it, and told me to reach inside. I did, and pulled out a small, pink child's jersey with Derek Lee's name printed on the back.

"This is for me?" I asked.

"Well, who else would it be for?" Dad gave a hearty laugh, and motioned for me to put it on. His expression was hopeful, yet almost defeated at the same time. So, without looking at my mother, I pulled the jersey over my head. Just as I finished adjusting it, we heard the cracking sound of ball smacking against a bat.

Like a reflex, our heads snapped toward the field as the Cubs fans stood up. Dad took me by the waist and lifted me up high above his head so that I could see over the rows in front of us. The ball soared out of the park, and the crowd chanted the batter's name as he rounded the bases to home.

I stole a glance at Mom, but her face was unreadable. She was still sitting, staring down at the shopping bag I had dropped.

"See?" Dad shouted to me. "What'd I tell ya? We can win games if we want to!"

I smiled down at him, and I wanted so badly to agree. I wanted to love baseball and enjoy it with my family. But, as always, I knew better.

Then, I had another thought: Baseball certainly wouldn't save us, but perhaps I could try liking it anyway. Dad set me down and I looked around Wrigley Field—that is, *really* looked. At the stands that seemed to rise up countless rows until they met the sky. At the thousands of fans who looked like a swarm of blue and white when you let them blend together. They were all here for one reason or another. Perhaps I could focus on my own reason, not Mom and Dad's.

So, as the summer drew to a close, I attempted to find one thing in Wrigley Field to admire each time we were there: the ice cream stands, the souvenir shop where Dad had bought my jersey, the balls that soared into the crowd. I kept this up until one particular Friday night game in late September. I was getting acclimated to junior high, but I was pleased to find it was easier to have conversations with the boys in my class, since we now had a shared interest. Relatively, at least. I thought it made me seem cool.

Mom was spending most nights we weren't at the games going over the family finances. Tonight, however, Dad wanted a beer, and she said no. It was his night to drive, she reminded him, and all I learned from that night was that alcohol somehow impaired your ability to use a car. Nothing about baseball.

Even without his drink, Dad went to use the restroom during the top of the sixth, like clockwork. I wished he'd stay this inning, seeing as we were winning this one. But, he'd told me it wouldn't matter. We were already second to last in our division and it was almost the end of the regular season. We hadn't won after all, and Dad had been out of work for several months at this point.

I turned to Mom. The thought had occurred to me mid-summer, but I wasn't sure how to voice it. Now, I decided, was the time to be blunt—when Dad wasn't here. "We could have just sold our season tickets, right?"

I had always assumed this comment would be an obvious observation, the kind that my parents had thought of months ago. But Mom looked taken aback. "Why would we do a thing like that?"

I paused before answering. "Money?" Season tickets had to be worth something.

Maybe Mom was late to this realization after all. Of course, she had thought baseball would save us, just like Dad did.

Mom shook her head. "Some things are more important than money, Maggie," she told me, patting my knee. Then, she fell silent.

By the time the game was almost over, Dad still hadn't plopped down in his seat next to me, readying himself for the next play he could attempt to explain. I glanced around our section, searching for his bright blue shirt in the crowd coming toward us—but there was no sign of him. Mom didn't say anything else to me for the rest of the game.

It was when Dad didn't come back, and the Cubs won, that I realized I wasn't ready for baseball to fail us.

We left Wrigley Field that night, Mom and I, like any other family. We sat in traffic, and when Mom tucked me in that night, she didn't ask how it felt to be a baseball fan.

In fact—and perhaps it was because our season tickets were up—she never took me to see the Cubs again.

* * *

The sixth inning arrives, and Cory leans over to whisper in my ear. "Wanna get out of here?" he asks, and it's a question I both anticipate and rejoice at.

"Sure." I smile, as though he hadn't known what my answer would be.

We stand up and I steal a glance at Keith. He's

still quiet, but seems a little more focused on the game. I don't think he's had a sip of beer in nearly ten minutes.

Once we're out in the walkways, I can still hear the cheering from inside the stadium. Each time I pass a snack stand on our way out, the monitors overhead inform us of who's up to bat.

"Just a baseball fan, huh?" Cory says, nudging me as we walk.

I grin. "So you were paying attention earlier."

But I choose to ignore his teasing. Yes, I'm only a baseball fan, nothing more. No team spirit, no blue, red, and white jersey for me. I slow down as we near another monitor, and then come to a complete stop. Cory stops with me, waiting. For several minutes, I listen to the cheers of the crowd inside and their reactions to plays we can no longer see in person. I'm not supposed to let myself stay this late into a game, so finally, I nudge Cory and we keep moving.

"Thanks for coming again tonight," I tell him, feeling a genuine smile form at my lips. I take his hand. "I appreciate it, even if you're not a fan."

His smile is serious. "I know it's hard being at these games. But the fact that you still go is amazing."

Nope, no team playing for me. But baseball itself? There's something different about it, different than what my parents saw within this stadium. They saw the pastime, the escape from reality. Instead, I see the reality, and I think I take comfort in that.

Tomorrow, Cory and I will return to our respective jobs—him to the bank and me to an advertising agency. And I'll find another game to go to within the next month or so. It's all I care to afford. Cory might come, or he might have better things to do.

"Mags! Hey, Mags! Wait!"

I spin around and notice Keith stumbling over to us.

"Shit," I mutter. I grab Cory's hand and start leading him more quickly toward the nearest exit. "C'mon, let's go."

But Keith already has his hand on my shoulder. He leans over and, for a moment, I think he's going to vomit on my shoes. Instead, he steadies himself, his hands on his knees. Breathes hard. As though it took all the energy in the world to chase after us. Maybe it did.

"I need to ask you something," he slurs out. "'Bout your dad."

"I don't think that's any of your business," I tell him sharply, and again take Cory's hand, trying to guide him to the exit.

"Wait—" Keith reaches out to me again, still sucking in air, and finally straightens. He looks me square in the eye, so focused that I almost believe the drunkenness is a charade. Luckily, I know better. I always do. "Did he ever give you season tickets?" he stutters out.

My eyes widen, but I'm not sure why. "What does that matter?"

Keith shakes his head as though I don't understand. I suppose I don't. "My old man, he got our family lifetime season tickets to the Cubs, right before he left us. We went to every fucking home game. Every fucking one, for years."

I eye Cory sideways; he nods, and I know he's

not going to let me leave just yet.

Keith keeps rambling on for a few moments, but I stop listening as I take in more of his appearance, now that we're face-to-face. He's even blonder than I realized. Platinum almost.

"So I want you to take them," he suddenly spurts out. Then, he shoves a tiny piece of paper into my hand. "My info, if ya want it."

My mother would say I was being rude for not listening. Avoiding her lectures is one of the things I value about not living with her anymore—but in times like these, perhaps it would be better to take her advice. I unwrap the folded paper and see a phone number and email address scrawled out on it.

"What did you say?" I almost don't want him to repeat himself.

"The season tickets. The ones my pop gave us," Keith urges. "I want you to take them."

I can't find the words to even garner a response. "Why on earth would you want me to take them?"

"'Cause I don't need 'em anymore. They make

me drink. They make me think of him." He pauses. "Why *do* you still come to these games? They make you better instead? Instead of what they do to me? That's sure what it seems like."

I actually stop and think for a moment. But not about his question; I'm wondering why I'm even having this conversation with a man who won't remember he offered the last remnants of his relationship with his father to a complete stranger. I can't let him do that, even if he doesn't have a team to cheer for anymore.

"I got a good feeling," he goes on. "About these next couple of years. The World Series. I really think it's is going to be our time soon—"

"You keep them, Keith," I interrupt him, and before I even know what I'm doing, I reach out and hand the paper back. "There's a reason you have them."

With that, I take Cory's hand and lead him away. This time, he follows.

* * *

Once Cory and I were engaged, back in November of last year, I went over to my mother's house to share the good news.

"As though I couldn't see it coming," she said, grinning as she leafed through some papers on the countertop in the kitchen.

Even though I was financially independent—could even help take care of her if she'd let me—Mom still preferred to freelance and work part-time.

"You want to tell your father, don't you." It was a statement, and Mom said it without looking up from her folders.

I pursed my lips. "No, I don't."

"You know what I found the other day?" she went on, not even missing a beat.

I held my hand out and busied myself with studying my new ring. I didn't normally wear jewelry, but I would be wearing this foreign object for the rest of my life. I hoped.

"I found that jersey he gave you, way back when," she said, not even waiting for me to prompt her. She knew I wouldn't, seeing as she probably thought I wouldn't like what she had to say. Even so, I was surprised when she smiled at this announcement. "It was in the closet upstairs."

"You said he shouldn't have bought it. Those genuine jerseys are overpriced. I'd never pay for one even now."

"You and I both know that's not the reason you don't have one these days." Her look was pointed, and I dropped my hand so I could focus more on the conversation I had fallen into.

"Why are you telling me this?" I asked her, and even though I knew the question would hurt, that I hadn't come over here to bring her more pain, but joy, I needed to know.

"I just thought you'd like to know it's here, that's all," she said. "That I still have it, if you want it."

"It won't fit me, and Lee hasn't been on the team in years. He doesn't even play anymore."

Mom straightened the last of her papers and stepped around the counter so that she could stand closer to me. "I know that."

I pushed back from my seat at the table. "When

we set a wedding date, you'll be the first to know." I gave her a quick smile and left.

I made my way out of Mom's quaint little house, back into my car and my world as it existed now. It was chilly, summer had long turned into fall, and I knew in a matter of months I'd be attending new games. Cory would come with me once in a while, and we would leave during the sixth inning. But I'd never buy myself season tickets, because that would mean I had a little too much faith in baseball.

No one should have that much faith in anything, I had decided long ago. It was better to simply look out for yourself.

As I drove, the trees rushed by in swirls of green, red, and yellow. Not pink and blue, like cotton candy. Once I rounded the last turn of Mom's subdivision, I thought about trying to call my father. Out of the blue, just like that. I thought about telling him the good news. That I hadn't failed. Yet.

I pulled my phone out at a stoplight, just blocks from the highway that would take me home to Cory. I keyed over to the most recent number I had for Dad—courtesy of the white pages—and thought about actually dialing. Then I thought about the jersey, the beer he always enjoyed, the money he had no problem spending. Perhaps in some other reality, if I let him help plan it, my wedding would be far more extravagant than it needed to be. I could joke about that for the time being.

I dropped the phone back into my purse without dialing and continued on my way. It was getting colder outside, but I kept my windows rolled down. I listened to the soft crackling of fallen leaves as the car's wheels drove over them, thought about how different this crackling sounded than a baseball hitting a bat. Thought that maybe I'd stop going to games from now on; take my nearly 500 and run. I wondered where I'd be when I was fifty, yelling at the television or watching my children grow up. Maybe I'd do both.

An unexpected detour took me off the highway and past Wrigley Field. The stadium had been empty for weeks, of course, as the Cubs hadn't made it to the postseason, and there was no other reason to use it this time of year. My windows were still rolled down, and as I drove by I looked out to my right, hearing the wind and cars zip by and pretending it was the crowd cheering inside. I prodded my imagination further, and saw a young girl who wore a pink Cubs jersey that matched the cotton candy she held in her hand. The jersey had to be pink; blue was for boys, she insisted.

I brought my foot down further on the gas and sped by the stadium, past the parking decks, past the memories, past that whole area of town that screamed baseball. I drove toward Cory, toward what was still unbroken, and the invisible crowd of 41,000 patrons roared after me. Their enthusiastic shouts followed me all the way home.

The New Ingredient

They're not here yet. I check my watch, then I check the clock on my cell phone, but the time doesn't change. It's still ten minutes until noon. Ten minutes until lunch time. Ten minutes until I get to see my daughter.

Violet sounded excited on the phone yesterday evening. I talked to her from the moment I set foot off the plane until I checked into my hotel.

"Daddy," she said excitedly. "We're bringing my new friend with us tomorrow! Mom said I could."

A new friend. To lunch. With a dad who hasn't seen his daughter in almost three months.

I try not to let the thought wrangle me too much, but it's tough. I've already been fired from my marriage. I don't need to be fired by my daughter, too. Mina would say I'm being ridiculous for thinking a friend is going to completely eat up the one afternoon I get with our daughter.

Well, I guess I'm ridiculous.

They agreed to meet me in the lobby at my hotel, and then we'll figure out where to go to eat. I sit with my legs crossed in an oversized armchair that I claimed near the reception desk. People wander in and out the front doors, bringing in the warm summer air and their complaints at the same time. Voices rise at the reception desk. Apparently the promised bottle of welcome champagne wasn't delivered to room 5310.

My thoughts return to Violet's new friend. I can't imagine why Mina would agree to let Violet bring someone along for the ride. Maybe it's meant to torture me. She would enjoy that...for a bit, at least.

The thought of Mina now makes my stomach churn. Her sly grins, the expressions she makes when she knows something you don't. Honestly, my entire marriage to her was torture. Until I wasn't married to her anymore. It's crazy what can happen when you leave for a three-week business trip and give your wife some time to rethink her life choices.

My phone vibrates and I snatch it up. *Running five minutes late.* From Mina.

I run my hand over my face and lean back in the armchair. Classic Mina: five minutes late. Classic me: twenty minutes early.

Voices rise at the reception desk again. The desk agent puts up his hands in an expressive *calm down* motion, and I watch as the hotel guests respond with their own set of hand gestures. I guess when you run out of people to yell at in your own life, you have to find some suitable alternatives.

My phone vibrates. Another text. *Violet's excited for you to meet her new friend. Be nice.*

What the hell is that supposed to mean? I shake my head, knowing that despite my greatest hopes, Mina can still see deep inside my thoughts. I almost despise her for it, but at times it brings a strange comfort.

I remember the first time I met Mina's "new friend." At least he's not supposed to be at lunch today. Though, knowing Mina, that could very well be changed.

But *he* doesn't bake with Violet.

He doesn't tell her stories late at night on the phone when Mina's asleep.

He isn't her dad.

I scroll through some photos on my phone while I'm waiting and pull up the last cake that Violet and I baked. It was for her eighth birthday, almost exactly three months ago. She was covered in chocolate icing and flour and insisted on licking all of it off, despite my objections. The cake didn't even turn out that great, but we ate it anyway.

Violet once told me on one of our secret late-night calls that she wanted me to move back home. That our two cities were too far apart. And that's true. They are too far apart.

So why is she bringing a friend to lunch?

The revolving doors at the entrance start moving, and my heart speeds up as two familiar figures walk through. The warm air fills the space again, just momentarily before the air conditioning takes over, and before I know it Violet's pressing herself into my arms.

Then something heavy lands on my lap.

I stare at the object for a few moments, then up at Mina. She shoots me her clever grin before coming up to give me a round-the-shoulder hug, as well.

"Meet my new friend, Daddy," Violet says, grinning ear-to-ear.

I hold up the heavy bag of flour and can't suppress my laughter. She's drawn a face on the back of it, and bits of white sputter out each time I move the bag even an inch.

"What is this?" I ask through snorts of laughter.

Then I remember Mina's words. *Be nice.* Violet's face falls.

I stare closely at the face she's drawn on the bag. At first it looked like a simple face, but now I notice the detail in the eyes, the pointed nose, the smiling mouth. She's even drawn freckles and lines where the faint wrinkles are supposed to be. It's... impressive.

And I'm relieved. I'm so relieved. I hug that bag of flour to my chest even though it covers my shirt in white dust as a result.

"It's nice to meet your new friend," I finally say, and it is.

The sunshine in Violet's face returns and I stand up to give her a proper hug.

We'll probably need a different bag of flour, but maybe she and I can bake a cake later.

For What It's Worth

I know absolutely nothing about the facts concerning the Russo-Japanese War. I don't know why it started, nor how it ended. In fact, I can only account for the obvious sides involved, and that it took place over a century ago. Yet I have never had a lesson on it. I've never opened my history textbook to a chapter that gleamed its name as the title. None of the battles that took place affect me, and the people involved are of little consequence to me. The Russo-Japanese War falls to the back of my mind but for one important fact: It's the reason I'm alive.

I grab a handful of rocks from the backyard and shove them into a plastic bag before meeting my family by the car. The cemetery is on the other side of town—or at least, it seems to be each time we've made the drive. It always proves difficult to find decent enough rocks to place on the tombstones when we're there, so I've made it my responsibility to supply some. Besides, there can't possibly be a more meaningful source of rocks than from your own backyard.

When we arrive at the cemetery, I take care to follow the adults in front of me. I look up and notice that the sun is fully exposed, casting shadows across the entirety of the grounds. I feel like somehow the sun is always shining when we're here. It reveals the undeniable age of many of the graves. I would get lost if I tried to find the correct spot on my own. There are some sorts of navigational features set into the pathways of the Orthodox cemetery, but I'm never inclined to try and understand them. Grandma Ruth's tombstone is at the opposite corner from where we entered. It's almost by the street. I could lean against the fence protecting it from the outside if I really wanted to. Instead, I stay still and just wait to hand out the rocks.

There's a rabbi with us, but it's fairer to say that he's a relative. He says a short prayer and conducts a quick service, honoring her *yahrzeit*. This is one of the few Jewish phrases that I really know: the anniversary of a loved one's death. Grandma Ruth died when I was twelve, just as I was starting to prepare for my Bat Mitzvah. Now it's been quite a few more years.

Kinehora means a "curse in reverse," an unjinxing of sorts. It's another Jewish word—a Yiddish one, actually. I don't understand much Yiddish. The word applies even to our lives outside of the Eastern European universe. We knock on wood, we cross our fingers behind our backs, or we simply say nothing that would require us to perform these actions. Over a century ago I suppose *kinehora* was a common term in Russia, in place of our Western superstitions. Over a century ago my great-grandmother was born into a culture that vehemently believed in bad luck. And unlike me, Ruth knew Yiddish.

I like to think back on reasons to be proud of my hometown of St. Louis, Missouri, the one that houses this old cemetery. 1904 was the year of the St. Louis World's Fair. The waffle cone was invented. It was an exciting period. Such excitement might have been the cause for Ruth and her family to leave Russia for the United States— and to ultimately arrive in St. Louis. Yet the World's Fair was not the source of the excitement that drew them. They immigrated not because of the buzz surrounding the waffle cone, but because of that war. They were following a loyal father, one who had fled to the States a couple years earlier to escape the draft.

Somewhere buried deep in my basement, there's a little cardboard shoebox decorated with pink and green construction paper on all sides. I'm not entirely sure where it is, but I know it has to be in one of those piles we like to put off sorting through. The box is probably covered in cobwebs and crawling with spiders by now. It was my third grade family history project. The most valuable component of the box, however, is no longer trapped inside. It's in our living room wall unit. I walk by it on a daily basis, and somehow it never catches my eye. It never serves to remind me why I'm here. It's just a photograph, and it's not even the original.

When I was in the third grade, I was excited to "interview" Grandma Ruth about her family so that I could in turn tell all my elementary school classmates. Having a grandparent that deep-rooted, with that much history, was certainly something I didn't mean to take for granted. But it didn't make me consider my roots from Russia. It was just cool. Even then, however, I still only felt like a St. Louisan. When my mother took my brother and I to Grandma Ruth's apartment to see her she was sitting in her normal spot, perched on the sofa next to the balcony door and across from the age-old television. She wore the same pink housecoat she liked to sport, and she had recently gotten her hair done. I could tell because the thinning strands looked fuller and not as wispy (but why she still saw a hairdresser, being over a hundred years old, I never understood). Many things I learned in the interview I already knew—she liked to talk about her family during any and all of our visits. So in reality, this was nothing special. But on this particular day, she showed me the photograph for the first time.

"My father hadn't seen us for a few years. It was so he would know us again," she explained.

Her family sent the photo to her father right before they left Russia. My mother went to get the original photocopied and laminated for me to bring to school, and while she did that I stayed with my brother and visited. Grandma Ruth's face glowed whenever she got an opportunity like this to spend time with us. She said to me on various occasions, including this one: "Well, you'll grow up to be beautiful and talented. *Kinehora.*"

Now our rabbi relative asks if anyone wants to share any memories they have of Ruth. I think back to this particular school project and say nothing. I look over at my mother. She doesn't look as though she wants to say anything either. I know she would have plenty to relate, if she really wanted to. She and Grandma Ruth had numerous comical rundowns that occurred between the two of them. The best was whenever they tried to bake together. But maybe here at the tombstone my mother keeps quiet because she thinks the family already knows these stories, and she doesn't feel like retelling any.

I certainly know the stories. When we weren't visiting Grandma Ruth to ask about her past memories, we were there to put her oven to work. Unfortunately, at my youthful age I was inclined to stay out of my mother and Grandma Ruth's "bonding" time. Instead, I kept to myself as they tried various recipes.

"We messed it up again," my mother had said tiredly on one of these occasions. "We used the garlic cooking spray instead of the regular."

I was sitting on the living room floor of Grandma Ruth's apartment, watching cartoons on the old television set as the two women attempted to make a Bundt cake.

"We did what?" Grandma Ruth asked in a louder tone than was necessary.

"We used garlic instead of regular!"

"Oh no, did we?" Grandma Ruth said laughing, and then as was custom, poured the rest of the ruined batter into the sink.

If messing up a recipe was considered taboo anywhere else, in our family it was tradition. My mother had learned to bake extremely well, and so had Grandma Ruth. Yet whenever the two of them were thrown into a kitchen together, something always went wrong.

"Gram, why don't you go take a rest on the couch while I clean up and get ready to start over?" my mother suggested in a loud, steady voice. "Go visit with the kids."

"All right," Grandma Ruth said, and took her walker from near the refrigerator—or as she called it, the "Frigidaire."

"What's on the television?" she asked me as she approached the sofa.

"Nothing much," I replied, and turned around to face the toy train set that rested nearby.

As was another visiting tradition, I would always run into Grandma Ruth's bedroom and grab the box underneath her chair that contained a multitude of toy train parts, before bringing them out to the living room. My brother was usually trying to fix something in the apartment that wasn't broken to begin with.

Grandma Ruth sat still for a second,

contemplating.

"Why don't you show me another dance?" she finally asked.

I always enjoyed relieving her of her feeling of immobility by giving a miniature showing of what I had done at the theater.

"Okay!" I said, standing up eagerly, and then prepared to enter from "stage right"—also known as the glass door that led to the balcony from behind the television.

I leapt back into the room, doing little turns and jumps and leaps, trying my best to remember every bit of choreography just as I had performed it. Whenever I did forget a move, I just made something up. She never noticed.

After I had finished dancing, Grandma muttered something in Yiddish under her breath. She had many Yiddish catch phrases, you could call them, and she used them consistently. Yet I never knew what they meant while she was alive, including *kinehora*. They were just things she always said. I also didn't realize that "Frigidaire" was actually a brand of refrigerators. I just assumed she didn't know how to say "refrigerator." In a way I was right.

My mother finally called her back into the kitchen. They were ready to attempt Round Two. Grandma Ruth's face was still beaming from watching me dance as she grabbed a hold of her walker and made her way back into the kitchen. I resumed playing with my trains and watching the boring cartoons. Grandma Ruth didn't have cable, but I managed to work with this particular drawback.

These days, I've taken up baking.

* * *

The small service is almost over and it's about time to dig into my bag of rocks. I stare ahead at nothing and think about what my parents will probably say to me in the car ride home. *You're so lucky to have known your great-grandmother for as long as you did.* Or it could be along the lines of: *You're going to have these wonderful memories forever.* The fact of the matter is, I know they're right.

It's strange to consider how some things stay in

one place for decades at a time, and then all it takes is a day or two before they disappear. I never knew Adam, Grandma Ruth's husband. I suppose I could call him my great-grandfather if I wanted to. I knew slightly more about my other set of great-grandparents, Abigail and Sam. We all have roots in St. Louis, dating back to when Grandma Ruth arrived. Turndale Lane was the best example of our lineage. It consisted of six fifties-style houses, three of which were inhabited by family: my great-Aunt Eileen and Uncle Gene lived in the one on the far right. The middle one was the home where my mother grew up. The one on the far left of the circle was where her grandparents, Abigail and Sam, lived. I came across Grandpa Sam's obituary recently, dated March 1995: "Samuel Turnstein, a longtime St. Louis contractor, died Saturday...of infirmities at the Westminster Retirement Home. He was 91." I barely knew him before he passed. He and Adam were the exceptions of the great-grandparents I remember so well. They both didn't live nearly as long as Grandma Ruth did.

Grandpa Sam had designed all six houses on

Turndale, which was then named after him. Most of our family gatherings would take place at Aunt Eileen and Uncle Gene's house. It was a small house, much like the others, but as the years went by only that house remained in our family. These get-togethers tended to get a bit stuffy for me, seeing as I was still pretty young. Up until my early teenage years, it was tradition to go over there for every large family occasion: Passover seders, Rosh Hashanah meals, or any other sort of celebration we happened upon. Their place consisted of a large living room, which blended into the dining room, with the kitchen in back. The bedrooms and Uncle Gene's office were scattered throughout the opposite end of the house. I used to take refuge over there whenever Uncle Gene scared me or scolded me—although I didn't quite differentiate between the two.

There was a piano against the wall of the living room, close to where we ate. I used to play it while the adults lounged around on the sofas and armchairs before dinner was ready. Grandma Ruth loved to hear me play. I was told that when

Grandpa Sam was alive he used to share the piano with me. There's even a "famous" photo of him sitting on the bench with both hands on the keyboard, while I sit next to him, keeping one hand beside his and holding my toy doll with the other. Unlike with Grandma Ruth's photograph, I have the original of this one.

Uncle Gene once told me that I was playing too loud, so I ran into the back bedroom, crying. I didn't come back until my parents coaxed me out to come eat. Grandma Ruth had always sat at the head of the table when dinner was ready, next to Uncle Gene. Seeing her there this time made me feel better. Gene was her oldest son. They shared the spotlight, it would seem.

When Grandma Ruth passed away, Uncle Gene followed the same year, and Aunt Eileen eventually sold the last Turndale house. We didn't go back to see that street for quite some time. It wasn't until only a few years ago at a small family gathering that we were passing around an article from the *St. Louis Post-Dispatch* with a picture of the neighborhood on it. The six homes were to be torn down, soon to be replaced with the types of houses you would find in any typical modern-day development. I heard these new homes were worth a fortune, and that many of the older houses in the surrounding neighborhoods would soon be meeting the same fate.

* * *

I pass around the rocks, and my relatives mumble their thanks as they prepare to approach Ruth's tombstone. Uncle Gene and Grandpa Sam's graves are not in this cemetery, I slowly realize, and I start to wonder why. But then I force myself to return my attention to the scene in front of me. My grandfather—Gene's brother and Ruth's younger son—bows his head slightly as he places his rock on the very edge of the solid structure. The rest of us follow. I can't help but feel a slight uneasiness as I put my rock down last. This always happens to me. It feels like everyone else is watching me, judging me. I didn't know her as long as they did. I don't know the meaning of this like they do.

Grandma Ruth kept the real photograph of her family in her apartment until she passed away. I'm actually not sure who has it now. But I know my own copy is still at home, preserved in the miracle of lamination. Right after she died I wished she could be preserved somehow, too. It wasn't until I was much older that I realized she was immortal in so many other ways. The videotapes we had of her at family gatherings, the birthday cards she sent us, the delicious recipes she left us with...they preserved her. Videotapes were especially important in our family. Before my mother moved out of her house on Turndale, years ago, she walked around with a video camera, filming each room and narrating where she was as she went. When I got the opportunity to watch it, I noticed her particularity as she described the various parts of her house. It seemed like something I would do.

Grandma Ruth lived by herself up until the week she died. Never did she stray away from that same spot on the couch when we arrived for a visit; never was she wearing something significantly different than that pink housecoat—and she always had a huge smile on her face. So few years ago I knew her like this. So few years ago I could have sworn I knew everything about her. I couldn't say that about Grandpa Sam. I couldn't say that about her husband Adam. And I still don't know anything about the Russo-Japanese War.

* * *

My mother and I had come by ourselves to Grandma Ruth's apartment shortly after her death, on the day we had to give up the keys. We found it empty, of course. The carpet was being replaced. I had never seen it like this, had never seen it without the old television set—or the sofa, or the dining room table.

My mother did her last sweep of the place, making sure nothing had been misplaced or forgotten. As she searched each drawer in the kitchen, pulling them out, checking, then looking in the next, I wandered back out to the living room. I stood in the area where I had played with the trains, watched television, and entertained

Grandma Ruth with my dancing.

I heard my mother's footsteps stop at the kitchen entrance, and she watched me for a moment.

"You know, the worst one was when the cake collapsed."

"Huh?"

"The Bundt cake. We took it out and tried to flip it over, but it pretty much imploded."

"Oh."

I was only twelve years old, but I was facing a forty-year-old's problem. Naturally, then, I dealt with it like any twelve-year-old would. It took years before my mother would watch any of those home videos we had of Grandma Ruth. I watched one the day of her funeral. That's what separated us, if I had to pin it down.

"Why don't you show her a dance from your recital?"

I looked back at my mother, letting the words seep in. If I danced right then and there, I would meet no applause, no beaming face, no compliments on what a "gorgeous, beautiful dancer" I was. When I finished there would only be an empty wall in front of me, and silence.

Our family has a habit of not letting go.

That video my mother made before she moved out of her house on Turndale wasn't very forlorn. She didn't cry as she held the camera. She simply talked to us, to whoever was listening. She knew she was making a memory that she would have forever. It was the same as how our relatives remained engraved in our memories. Her last line before turning off the camera was simple, but striking: "Say *buh bye!*"

It may seem odd, but Grandpa Sam would likely have said the same thing. The piano-playing, intuitive home contractor would have perhaps just considered the move as completing one project, while being hopeful of starting another. But no one wants to say another goodbye here, as we linger by the gravestone in the Orthodox cemetery, thoughts of leaving only latent in our minds. For what it's worth, not finding a personal value in my relatives' histories probably just means that I've found more value in my own. That's not really saying goodbye.

Maybe if I'm lucky I'll grow up to be over a hundred years old just like Grandma Ruth, to see my great-grandchildren grow up to be early teenagers, to get to bask in the joy that comes with being part of a family for just a little while longer.

Kinehora.

Partition

The bathroom stall has always been your safe haven. In the midst of a brain-crushing, sanity-shrinking workday you're always able to come in here, sit, and think for a moment. Not a bad deal, either: you get some privacy and quiet without having to fight for it—everyone uses the bathroom at some point, of course. No one would suspect you're using it to your full advantage.

Back in grade school, you used to run into the bathroom stall whenever Bobby Gerstein pulled your hair and grabbed the potato chips from your lunch bag. It always had to be your lunch. He was short and chubby, and everyone said he liked you. You started to think so, too, until that day in middle school when he got a girlfriend and continued to punch your shoulder with his backpack whenever he passed by in the hallway.

Bobby Gerstein ended up getting his stomach stapled almost twenty years later. He got just a bit *too* chubby.

You sit back and take in the tall partitions surrounding you. It's warmer here than in the office, which you appreciate. It's always so cold at your desk. You enjoy the privacy—the intimacy—of being walled off from the rest of the building bustling around you for just a few moments. You appreciate the break. You need it, after what happened earlier with Jay.

It wasn't your fault—not that it's anyone fault. But it wasn't yours. That much is for certain. Working in a tight cubicle where socialization is somewhat limited and people tend to grow bored is just a part of life. And when Jay decided to be bored by your cubicle, you couldn't help but pay attention.

Bobby Gerstein always insisted he wasn't eavesdropping on you at lunch as you chatted with your friends, you suddenly remember. He'd just take your chips and leave.

It was the same case with Jay—not that you mean to compare this to grade school, though in a sense Jay was acting like a child and you couldn't really leave your desk...except to use the bathroom, you suppose.

But even after he made off with your chips, Bobby Gerstein would sit at the next table, his curious eyes fixated right on you.

Jay had been standing by the copier behind your cubicle when he started the conversation with Aaron, another basic coworker employed at will, just like you. But there was nothing basic about the conversation, especially when the words "cheated" and "my wife Dani" were used in the same sentence.

You almost did a double take, but the opening behind your cubicle wasn't entirely private, and you knew they might notice the sudden movement. But why, of all places, would they have this conversation here?

"How are you feeling?" you heard Aaron ask Jay. As if that mattered. He had cheated on his wife, supposedly. You hadn't heard the entire ordeal. But if that was the case, there were only a few emotions he could be feeling right now: guilt, for being disloyal; relief, for finally getting something out of his system; or a very strange but delicate combination of the two.

But again, it didn't matter, and now as you sit in your "unofficial cubicle," cast away from the day and the drama and the sunlight streaming in through the windows, you can't help but be thankful that Darren isn't like that.

Darren. He's no Bobby Gerstein (thank goodness). You could handle it if he were heavy, like Bobby, but the comparison comes more from personality. Darren is...uncommon. Uncommon in the way you would describe a dog that doesn't like chasing squirrels. Typical male characteristics are overrated to him. He just...is.

So why have you been feeling terrible ever since you overheard Jay and Aaron? You're an intuitive person; maybe you were empathizing too much. This is why you shouldn't eavesdrop, though it wasn't your fault, you remind yourself again.

You've been in the stall for about five minutes

now.

It's a fairly big bathroom. The office building is large and no one notices who comes and who goes since there are so many stalls available. Maybe you can afford a few more minutes of quiet.

Dani...Dani and Jay. Their names sound nice together, and you suddenly hope it will work out for them. Maybe Jay just had a drunken night out over the weekend with his friends and kissed a girl for a few seconds. Maybe he's thinking of "emotional cheating" and was caught looking at porn. Regardless of what really happened, you wish that was it.

The bathroom door opens and in comes a set of high heels tapping against the tile floor. You sit back, almost as though whoever walked in is going to knock on your stall door and demand you get back to your cubicle.

You hear the newcomer enter a stall a few doors down from you, and the door locks with a satisfactory click.

Honestly, you're a little disappointed that no one has come looking for you.

You begin to wrap up and leave the stall at the same time this woman does. You both smile at one another, and you recognize her from the fifth floor. She's an accountant, if you recall correctly. Definitely not basic like you, the simple administrative assistant.

As you return to your desk, you notice Jay in the opposite corner of the office. He's no longer talking to Aaron, which comes to you as a relief, but he's still not at his cubicle. He looks rather hopeless, if you stare at him long enough.

On your desk is a photo of Darren. He's very happy to be with you, so you should probably continue being thankful that he's yours. But you can't, because you know not everything is okay.

Dani and Jay. You and Darren. It all flows so well, and yet none of it is right. You stand up at your cubicle, but the partition is a bit too tall to spot Jay from overhead. You sit and scoot your desk chair backward instead, through the opening, and lean back as though you're stretching. That's not suspicious at all, given that you just spent nearly ten minutes in the bathroom and had plenty of time to stretch your legs.

You have half a mind to talk to Jay, but you shouldn't. Instead, you wheel yourself back in and stare at Darren's photo yet again. He wants to take you hiking next weekend. It's a very sweet gesture, given that he normally doesn't enjoy it very much.

You rest your head in your hands and breathe deeply. No, you shouldn't talk to Jay. Instead, you should probably talk to—

Your phone buzzes next to your elbow. It's a text message, and every piece of you wants it to be from Darren. You want him to check in on you. To simply say hello. That's all you need right now.

But the message is not from him, and your heart rate increases as you open it.

DANI: Did you make up your mind about us yet?

Just as quickly as you scan the words, you flip your phone over so the screen is facing the faux wood of your desk. Not that anyone can see into your cubicle anyway.

Once your heart calms down a bit, you decide you need an emergency bathroom break. Ignoring anyone who might notice you leaving again, you hurry past the long line of desks and out the door. Down the hall. Into the bathroom, where it's warmer and private and even the truth is something that can wait for a few more minutes.

Empty Cities

The pavement was cold under Thomas's sock. He had slipped off his right shoe when no one on the platform was looking and began tracing the ground with the ball of his foot. Side to side. Forward and back. It reminded him of when he was a child, always interested in removing some article of clothing when his mother wasn't looking. When she finally noticed, she would snatch him by the hand just before he took off something that he probably shouldn't. Thomas smiled at the memory.

As someone approached his bench, he shoved his foot back into his dress shoe and adjusted enough to make it seem as though he were merely stretching. The woman who sat down barely glanced in his direction, immersed in a magazine she held in her hands. Thomas attempted to profile her out of the corner of his eye, but his peripheral vision didn't fare well behind his thick-rimmed glasses. The woman sat further into the bench and crossed her legs. Deciding she was no longer interesting to him, Thomas looked toward the other benches scattered about the station. Each one had two or three people occupying it: men, women, children, the elderly—in any given combination.

Thomas's first instinct was to find an empty bench somewhere nearby so he could have his space back, but he figured that doing so would look rude to the woman next to him, and he probably wouldn't be able to find an unoccupied bench anyway. He had come at the busiest time of the evening—and during the Christmas holiday travel week, if it weren't already enough. It had only been a few hours since his conference ended and he was released from his business endeavors to travel back home. He couldn't have left the hotel fast enough, but realized soon after that it probably meant waiting at a busy train station for quite some time until his scheduled line showed up. The hotel hosting the conference had been too stuffy, full of people just like him. It wasn't the type of company he cared to associate himself with too much.

The ground shook as the sound of an arriving train grew louder. Just when Thomas looked up to identify its destination, the woman next to him stood and threw aside her magazine. It remained open to the same page she had left it.

Thomas refrained from picking up the magazine, though he was looking for a way to pass the time. Boredom could keep him for a little while longer. The train that the woman had just disappeared onto continued to board more and more people who appeared out of nowhere. The platform grew emptier in segments, but then was re-inhabited just as quickly. The flow of people never stopped.

A breeze from above the platform covering reached the bench and flipped over a few pages of the magazine, drawing Thomas's eye back to it. He scanned the crowd, checking to see if anyone was heading close to him, before snatching the magazine and opening it to a random page.

He glanced up as the train started moving, an eyebrow raised. The exhaust of the train's engine invaded the air before the train reached a quicker speed and began its journey from the station to God-knows-where.

Thomas had never heard of the publication he held in his hands; being called *The Northeast Quarterly*, he could only draw conclusions as to why. It sounded boring. And educating.

Now, as he sat alone in his secluded spot at the station, maybe it was time to become boring and educated—though, he had boring down rather well already. He flipped through the magazine until he landed on a self-help article written by someone named Brenda Marks. She would probably call him boring, too, if she knew him. Took one to know one, he supposed.

Their names were all the same, these female writers: Brenda, Lauren, Julia, Gail...

Trish.

They sounded the same and wrote the same material. They wrote about how family breakups were always the men's fault—that they didn't care for their wives and children and always acted in a destructive way toward the family, leading to eventual divisions. Thomas flipped to another article. It was about a family that had started a local bakery and worked their way up from nothing. Everything in there was local, and that was the problem. Everything landed too close to where he sat at this very moment.

But then again, those families hadn't experienced the night that changed everything. Not his, at least.

Thomas threw aside the magazine, drawing his hat further over his forehead so that he could cover his eyes more than his glasses already did. He didn't want to observe the other benches anymore. He didn't want to stare because, now, they all looked like families—like happy, put-together families.

A middle-aged man, probably a few years older than him, settled next to him on the bench.

"Been pretty busy around here," the man commented, crossing his legs and unfolding a newspaper. He paused before looking at Thomas.

"Where you headed?"

"Pittsburgh," Thomas replied, a blank stare on his face.

The man took this curt response as an initiative for more conversation.

"I'm headed up to Boston. Meetin' some relatives there for the holidays. Pittsburgh your home?"

"Yeah."

"Haven't been there too often. My daughter went to Penn State, but I was never really around that region much to begin with. Nice programs, though. You got kids?"

Thomas looked up and met the man's eyes for the first time since he had sat down. The man had a gentle expression that revealed far too much. He was certainly a family man, probably closer to retiring than Thomas was. He was going to visit relatives up north...and he was most likely a good father.

"I, uh, yeah. I have...just one." Thomas's voice nearly caught as he mumbled his reply.

"Son or daughter?"

Thomas noticed he was fidgeting and clasped his hands together to stop. "Daughter."

"She got a name?"

"Adeline—I mean, uh, Addie. She goes by Addie."

The man nodded, smiling to himself. "How old is Addie, then?"

Thomas thought for a moment before answering. "She'll be eighteen in three weeks."

"Wow, so you're coping with that whole empty nest syndrome, eh? She started college this fall?"

"Yeah."

"Where at?"

It was people like this man who defined Thomas. They defined him by representing who he wasn't. He was more like the men at his conferences who were always away from their families on business trips, who could barely make it home in time for the holidays. Thomas wondered if this man with whom he found himself talking had taken off work to be with his family in Boston. He had half a mind to ask—this man had taken the liberty to ask him all sorts of questions, after all.

Thomas had encountered people like him before. He didn't ask, though. He only answered him with a lie of his own.

"Ohio State." It was his alma mater.

"And you're from Pittsburgh, you said?"

"Yeah, that's right."

The man chuckled. "At least she didn't go all the way to California."

Thomas didn't respond. The man took up his newspaper in good time and began musing over the editorials. Thomas redirected his stare to the far end of the platform, left of his bench. Down there stood a large Christmas tree. Its ornaments gleamed against the darkening surroundings, and many passersby stopped for a few short moments to admire its beauty or comment on its decorations. But this was only in passing, as they had better places to be. That's why they were here, of course.

The temptation to walk over and admire the tree was high now, but Thomas held back. He imagined staring into one of the round, colorful plastic ornaments. He visualized seeing not his reflection in the glare, but *hers*.

Trish's image startled him, but Thomas wasn't going to give her a victory today.

The man next to him had grown quiet, so Thomas absentmindedly picked up the magazine again. He flipped through the pages until a slight pounding began in his head; he reached inside his briefcase to grab a bottle of over-the-counter painkillers he'd picked up earlier, popping a couple into his mouth before swallowing them dry. The pain didn't go away in that instant, and he didn't think he could look at that magazine much longer. He tossed it into the trashcan next to his feet.

In good time the other man left, when the train bearing the sign BOSTON came rumbling into the station. The man bade Thomas a goodbye and a happy holiday before dropping his newspaper into a recycling bin and wheeling his suitcase toward the boarding platform.

The sky was dark, as Thomas could see through the covering, and the station had begun emptying out. The rush had passed, but his train still wasn't due for about an hour. He considered grabbing a coffee and newspaper from the nearby café, but decided he'd rather stick with his bench.

Eighteen, he thought. How could she possibly be eighteen now? He had only seen her, what, seven times since the split? Addie had been about eight on that terrible night—the night that had thrown Thomas so off course. She was nine when the divorce was finalized. The last time he saw her, she was probably around ten or eleven years old.

The amount of contact he kept with them and the value he held of his visitation rights had dwindled after his first couple of years alone— when his child support went on without acknowledgment. He might as well have tossed the money down a well; he would never see it again anyway.

Thomas couldn't help but wonder about her— about them—at times. He knew Trish was now remarried, that she was happy being out of Pittsburgh, restarting her life. Then, there was Thomas, stuck within a world of business trips and empty apartments filled with nothing but outdated photographs.

It took too much energy to be mad, and Thomas had decided long ago that he wasn't anymore. The energy had since converted into nostalgia. He missed her. He missed his daughter. He missed Addie.

The Christmas tree taunted him again. No one on the platform stood between his bench and the symbol of the holiday. He could see it in its full glory, even from strides away. He wanted to walk over to it, to take in its image and meaning, but he couldn't bring himself to stand. He didn't have a Christmas tree back home in his apartment. He hadn't bothered with the ordeal for years. Thomas peered over the top of the trashcan, where he had tossed in the magazine. Someone had just walked by and dropped a Styrofoam cup filled with coffee into it, and that put an end to his temptation to become educated and read it all.

Trish and Addie probably had a fresh Christmas tree every year in their new home. A live one. Not plastic, like the same one Thomas had carted out of the basement each year. A live, full-grown breathing tree—like the one in the station.

"All you had to do was go out one night and buy one. It wouldn't have taken long at all. Just put it up and let us decorate it."

He remembered Trish telling him this, her words crisp and clear as though she had just spoken right next to him. Was that all he needed to do for them to stay?

The Boston train released its engine exhaust before it, too, disappeared from the station. It would be less than an hour now until the Pittsburgh line arrived. His bench was empty, he had all of his things with him, and the dark sky was somewhat soothing.

No, he reasoned. Buying a live Christmas tree wouldn't have kept Trish and Addie around.

He thought back to the conference. Yes, everyone there was just like him, leaving their families at home for their business trips during the Christmas holiday. But he took the cake. He still attended even without a family to leave behind. He was years ahead of them all. Now such conferences were all he had left. He should have shouted out to the others there: *"Look at me! Look at what I did!*

Don't do the same thing. Don't make that same mistake. Go back to your families. Go home."

At that thought, Thomas sat up straighter; the truth was a distant enemy of his, always ready to make an appearance when he wanted it least. But, he wouldn't give the truth a victory today, either.

A teenage girl approached his bench and sat down. Thomas didn't look at her. She didn't attempt to talk to him, as the previous man had. She seemed somewhat reserved, and kept to herself. Thomas couldn't really think of anything else to do, so he slipped off his shoe and began running it across the pavement again. At this point, he didn't care if the girl noticed.

She did notice, however, and seemed trapped in a gaze as she watched his foot glide against the concrete. He knew she was watching—that much his poor peripheral vision allowed him to discern, but he still said nothing. Then, the girl slipped off her own shoe and began mimicking his movements. She moved her foot in the same direction as his, before taking off on her own and tracing the shape of a figure eight.

"I used to do this as a kid," she finally said, giggling a bit.

Thomas didn't say anything at first. He still hadn't looked over to see who she was in detail. He could only tell from his glances that she was younger.

She seemed embarrassed by her comment in the next moment, so she slipped her shoe back on and returned to her silence. Thomas, as much as he resisted, couldn't help but feel as though he should respond. She was just a kid—despite the fact that she said she *used* to be one.

"I did a lot of weird things as a kid," he said. "This was one of them."

She looked over at him, smiling. "Yeah, you were probably one of those kids that didn't enjoy shoes?"

Thomas chuckled, slightly pleased at her perception. "Pretty much."

The girl nodded. "So, where are you going?"

Thomas had grown accustomed to this question and answered almost before she finished asking. "Pittsburgh. Home."

"What were you doing out here?"

"I was on a business trip."

"Oh, gotcha."

The girl crossed her legs and sat up straighter. She tucked a piece of hair behind her ear and looked over at him again.

"So you live in Pittsburgh?"

"Yep."

"I have family in Pittsburgh. Distant family."

At this, Thomas finally eyed her up and down. She had dark, curly hair and pale skin. Such a stark contrast. "Oh yeah? You visit there often?"

"No, not really. I don't get to travel that much, honestly. My mom's a bit overprotective, you know?"

"Yeah, I know the sort," Thomas mumbled. He moved so that he was crossing his legs, as well. "So, what were you out here for?"

"Visiting some friends from college."

"I see."

Thomas thought back to the place he would be bound for in just a few short moments. He would board the train only to be transported back to an empty city, void of any sort of spirit of family. He found it hard to look at the girl now. She felt so familiar, like a part of him he no longer knew. He didn't dare ask her name. He hoped she wouldn't be forward enough as to ask for his. She was probably just the type to enjoy short-term company, no matter whom she found herself with.

It was impossible, he reasoned. This wasn't Addie. Despite his lack of recent photographs at home, despite Trish's efforts to sever all contact between them, he would know her face, her voice.

I'm not a bad guy, he told himself. *I hope Addie realizes that.*

The girl hadn't spoken again. She probably noticed Thomas deep in thought, and didn't want to disturb him. Thomas knew he could easily end the conversation here, but something was prodding him forward. He suddenly yearned for that connection with her, with anyone now for that matter.

Thirty minutes to board.

"So, you're not spending the holidays with your friends?" he asked her.

She shook her head. "Mom wanted me home. She likes the whole family being together for Christmas."

"Right. Well, that makes sense."

"It can be annoying, I guess," the girl went on, "but she always tells me I'll have plenty of opportunities to do what I want when I'm older. For now, she likes me at home."

"Empty nest syndrome?" The phrase felt unnatural coming from Thomas's lips.

"Yeah, you could say that," the girl replied, grinning. "Do you have kids?"

It was almost as bad as her asking his name. Thomas uncrossed his legs and spread his fingers out over his knees.

"Yeah, I ha-have a daughter. She's almost eighteen."

"Still in high school?"

"No, college freshman."

"So that means she's around my age."

"Yep."

"Where does she go to school?"

It was harder to lie to her than it had been with

the man. "Ohio State."

"Good school, good football team, as much as I hate to admit."

"Why, where do you go?" he asked her, feeling a sudden eagerness to find out.

"Miami of Ohio, actually."

Thomas found himself smiling. He had been close in his guess. It also didn't take him long to realize how dangerously close this girl was to making that possibility a reality. It couldn't be her. He didn't want to know if it was. He did feel a sudden craving for coffee, though.

He stood abruptly and mumbled something about the café before heading off in that direction, even further away from the Christmas tree. He hoped so fervently that she would be gone when he returned—that her train, wherever it was headed, would disappear, taking her far away from him. He leaned against the counter inside the station café as they brewed his cup, images of Trish and his young daughter soaring through his mind. It took both hands to steady himself against the counter before he could reach up with one hand and take his drink. The cashier behind the register looked slightly concerned and offered him some water, which he declined. He wanted to stay inside the café just long enough to be sure she was gone, but he knew if he did he might miss his own train.

A departure announcement came over the intercom inside, announcing the arrival of the line bound for Indianapolis. Hoping that would be hers, Thomas sat at one of the café tables for a few more minutes. His heart was beating at a pace it wasn't quite used to—at least, not in recent years. As he visualized this girl's face, visualized his daughter's, he knew where the victory would go today.

But perhaps his distant enemy could also be his friend.

Thomas remembered sitting with Addie in her bedroom the same day Trish threw him out, awkwardly stroking her back as she cried. She had a tendency to get upset whenever he and Trish fought. But this fight was different. This fight had ended them all. He looked Addie in the eyes and was about to say something—anything—to make the situation better, when she interrupted him. Her tearstained face spoke louder than her words.

"Daddy, I miss my brother."

Statistics did say that marriages were more likely to fail after the death of a child. And that terrible night, Thomas did anything but look up statistics. Instead, he let his emotions go. Disappear. He surrounded himself with emotionless people at work, where there was no reason to show interest, or passion, or love.

Brenda Marks was right. Those types of men didn't deserve family.

Thomas headed back outside to the platform. To his dismay, the girl was still at the bench. He lingered a little before deciding there would be no way for her to miss him walking by. He walked slowly toward the bench and sat back down.

"Coffee any good?"

"Decent enough." There it was. His stoicism.

The girl looked at her watch. "My train should be here in a few minutes."

Thomas took a prolonged sip of his coffee and didn't reply.

The girl stared across the empty train tracks.

Thomas snuck another glance at her as she zoned out on the open space. She didn't seem very pleased, relieved, or anywhere near excited for that train to come. She almost looked upset.

"Is Christmas your favorite holiday?" he asked.

He wasn't sure why he wanted to know this, or if he even desired to know this. Something about her blank expression just made him uncomfortable.

She shook her head. "No, I don't think so."

"Why not?"

She didn't answer right away. "I don't know, I mean, it's great to see everyone in my family. I just don't feel like it's the type of holiday that completes me, you know?"

"Completes you?"

"Yeah, like, makes me feel full, excited. It hasn't been like that for a while."

It was strange that she was telling him this so freely. He imagined her sitting in the same position she sat in now, only inside an office, positioned opposite a man with a clipboard. Was he just like that man?

No, he decided. He couldn't feel anything

anymore. He'd never become someone like that.

"So, what is your favorite holiday?" he went on.

"I'm not sure. I like Thanksgiving. The food is great. I like Easter, too."

"Okay, then."

"And Mother's Day."

Thomas looked up. "Why Mother's Day?"

"Because I love gift-giving, and I like when I can make my mom happy."

"Is she happy?"

The girl gave him a sideways stare when he asked this. Thomas immediately sat further back into the bench and said nothing. He realized how odd it had sounded, even after all the girl had told him already.

"I mean—"

"No, I understand. We're great."

He wasn't sure what to make of her response, but prodded no further.

The familiar low rumbling in the ground shot up through his feet all the way to his head. Another train was on its way. Thomas figured his wasn't due for at least ten more minutes.

The girl stood up and adjusted her jacket.

"It was nice talking to you," she told him, grinning. "I hope you have a great holiday with your family."

He nodded, fidgeting with his fingers again. This time, he didn't attempt to stop.

The girl grabbed the handle of her suitcase and began wheeling it toward the boarding platform as the train emerged from the tunnel. Thomas refused to look at the sign at the front of the train, announcing its destination. He couldn't.

He thought of Addie, wondering where she was right now, what she was doing, what she was thinking. He thought of Trish, and her determination to surround their daughter with love. His memories invaded his mind all at once, the image of Trish slamming the front door in his face, calling him out for not putting his family first anymore. Too many business trips, not enough time for dinner, or the holidays, or Addie's dance recitals.

Anything to avoid showing his love for them both. Because any moment they, too, could slip away.

The release of exhaust from the train engine pulled him from his thoughts. Thomas looked around haphazardly, taking in his surroundings. The station was virtually empty, with no one in sight. Most people were boarding the train that the girl had disappeared onto. His eyes were drawn to the door she had entered. It was right near the front. The sign at the head was still taunting him, gleaming its neon letters for him to see. The destination, the place this train was taking her to. It was right in front of him. It could be the same place.

Thomas glanced once more at the Christmas tree. It looked forlorn in the emptying station, as though it needed people around it in order to appear cheery. Young Addie would have loved it. He wondered if she still would.

Thomas couldn't take it any longer. He looked at the sign on the train. In an instant his eyes widened.

Without a moment's hesitation, he stood up. He was walking before he realized his feet had moved.

He hurried toward the boarding platform, hoping that no one would notice. Then he froze, only a few yards from his bench. His eyes focused on that same door, on that one threshold he could cross if he so chose to, even if only for a few minutes. A few minutes would be all he needed to ask for her name.

To ask for her name, and to wish her a Merry Christmas.

"Don't look too good or talk too wise."

I've always loved Halloween. I like the feel of it, the fallen leaves that soar through the air as cars and people rush through them. Even the crispness of the air doesn't usually bother me. I've never minded the cold, but when I was younger, my mother always made me wear a jacket and leggings under my costume before I went trick-or-treating. That was a feeling I didn't enjoy. If she were here tonight, I could hardly believe she would have recommended anything different for my cheap, revealing cowgirl costume.

Now as I stand here in the midst of the freezing night, years beyond begging for candy, I watch partyers dressed head-to-toe in costumes while they stumble up and down the block—and I can't help but wonder if this is considered normal. It depends on how you define the word. Normal could mean something you're used to, something you have always observed. My childhood Halloweens back home were normal in that way. Or, normal could refer to what is seen by society as ordinary, but not necessarily by the individual. By that definition, being stuck at a block party with a group of inebriated college friends makes me long for the feeling this night used to give me.

I can't stand in the chilliness much longer; my exposed legs shake visibly, and my arms are folded tight across my chest as I hug myself. Someone runs down the street and bumps into my shoulder as he passes us, forcing me to unwind. I feel a rush of cold air, and I immediately replace my arms. Melissa, Rebecca, and our other friends start moving, so I follow. I think Melissa needs a bathroom, and is investigating the houses on the block to see if she can find one. The entire street has been closed off for the party, and no one here seems normal to me. It's a hard test to pass, that of normalcy, seeing as I don't consider drunkenness to be in that category.

I'm fairly certain I'm the only one who's sober. But I'm not a good judge. Melissa points to another house, but its front door is closed. We go around the side and I watch as a few girls in our group attempt to climb a small fence to get into the yard. I see the backdoor is open. It might mean a bathroom for them. Almost every one of them has made it over when they look at me expectantly. I back off. They look unsurprised. I must, too.

* * *

Many Halloweens ago, when I was around four or five, I might have been more cunning than I am now. Whether it was a holiday or not, I was always able to plan and execute a way to get where I wanted to be. There was a child gate in my bedroom doorway that closed me off from the rest of the house at night. It was supposed to keep me from running into the hallway as a toddler and falling down the stairs.

My mother would tell me frequently, years later, that she was quite convinced I would do time. I was too cunning. I wondered if she meant it, if she joked about it with her friends because she thought her dark prediction might come true. This seemed like a reason *not* to joke about it. Perhaps she recalls it now, only because she can do so from the safety of knowing it's never happened.

According to her, I must have been sitting up in bed on my fourth or fifth Halloween, far past the time I should have been asleep, staring at the gate, wondering what I was missing on the other side. I slid out from under my sheets and crawled to the door, where the gate fenced me in. I sat with my back against it, looking around my room, thinking. I grabbed the trashcan first, based on the evidence my mother found later. It was the sturdiest. I turned it over and placed it against the center of the gate. Then I found my little play chair from the tea table in the corner. That went next. But soon I realized it was sturdier than the trash can, so I reversed their placement and put the chair underneath. I stepped onto the chair and began to balance myself on the trashcan. I could almost reach the top.

I checked my room once more, like a manager checking his inventory. I spotted a few board game boxes by my bed, scurried over to them, and added them to the stack. Quickly and without much noise, I hoisted myself up and over the gate. I landed with a soft *thud* on the carpet in the hallway. I looked around, content. I wasn't sure where to go now, what to do, what could be explored. It was my house after all; I had been everywhere before. I crawled to the top of the staircase. The light from the bathroom behind me only reached halfway down the bannister. The staircase culminated at the bottom in one great, black abyss. I was intrigued.

* * *

Melissa and Rebecca have made it into the house. I stick around outside, attempting to ignore my chills but distracted by them all the same. I try to control my shock at how everyone just climbed the fence. I've never seen girls our age do something like that. I take into consideration their current inebriated state, but it's still a strange thing to witness. The fence is probably twice the height as my child gate was. I don't step any closer to it. It's metal; it looks like it could prick straight through my skin, pierce my denim cowgirl skirt. It's not meant to be climbed.

I think about this past summer when I took charge of cleaning out our basement. I found the child gate leaning against our old trampoline that probably should have been thrown out two yard sales ago. As I stood against the gate, I realized how tall I was now. I could almost step over it without even going on tiptoe. It must have looked like a giant to me when I was five, just like this fence in the yard does now. But I'm not a climber anymore.

* * *

As I emerged from the darkness of the downstairs hallway, I found myself in the kitchen. The light was on over the sink, and I felt relieved to be out of the obscurity that was the rest of the house. I remembered that my mother had put some candy in the cabinet next to the microwave, leftover from trick-or-treating that day. I wasn't supposed to have any more that night.

I hurried to the kitchen table and pushed one of the chairs over to the counter. My climbing skills had been warmed up by then, and with surprising ease I pushed myself onto the counter itself. I stood up and opened the cabinet, the slight fear of falling disappearing quite rapidly as I found my treasure. There it was: a bowl of candy left just where I thought it was. I fingered through it and picked out a few chocolates and some fruit snack wrappers. Then I sat down on the counter, swinging my legs back and forth as I enjoyed the unexpected treat and listened to the quiet of the house.

* * *

Melissa comes stumbling out the front door. I don't see them from the backyard. I happen to look left and see Rebecca following her, so I run to catch up. I feel uncomfortable admitting it to myself, but they might have otherwise forgotten and left me. All I want to do now is go back to my dorm. I want pull on a pair of pajamas, microwave a frozen meal, and sit in bed with the television on.

But I can't leave the group. I don't even know how to get home, and I don't know who else would be in good enough shape to walk with me. We're close enough to campus. But I'm stuck wandering with them until they, too, tire out and want to leave. The block doesn't seem to end, but somehow we finally reach the last house. I feel a slight relief, until Melissa motions to the group and we start walking back in the direction from which we came.

I'm on a search for normalcy, and I'm not finding it anywhere. The fronts of the houses glow, but not in the ways I remember, like at home. They don't glow because of the line of carved pumpkins set up and down their lawns. The glowing comes from lighters being passed around from smoker to smoker instead. The blinking lights inside are not welcoming; rather, they send a message to go away. I was always told never to enter anyone's home when trick-or-treating, and each time I cross a threshold in this neighborhood tonight, into these widely-deemed "open houses," I wonder if it should feel ordinary.

I never would have thought about coming to a party like this a year ago. My mother always tells me what a difference a year makes, and I think about that now. What an incredible amount of change one person can go through, that makes you so different from October of one year to October of the next.

So it's logical to also consider how much of a difference ten years can make, or fifteen, or twenty. Even something as small-scale as six months, a week, five minutes. Anything can happen in any amount of time that can change you.

I don't know what has changed me, from age five to now. I still like chocolate; I still like Halloween. But I won't climb a fence anymore.

* * *

I threw away the candy wrappers and made it upstairs without disrupting anyone in the house. Realizing I had nothing to climb over to get back inside my bedroom, I hurried into the bathroom and immediately returned with the little blue plastic trainer toilet I used to occupy rather frequently. I dropped it onto the floor against the gate and climbed up, reaching as high as I could to pull myself up and over. The frame wobbled a bit as I forced my weight on it. It was only made of wood after all, with plastic-covered wires forming the middle.

With one swift movement, the gate steadied and I tumbled onto the other side, knocking over the chair and the board games and the trashcan. I rolled over on my back, staring up at the ceiling. I smiled. I still tasted the chocolate in my mouth.

* * *

I want to leave the block party. I want to be surrounded by the warmth of my own bed, the covers pulled tightly over my body. I don't even need the frozen food anymore. I just want to go home.

Melissa, Rebecca and the other girls choose

another house. Someone else needs the bathroom. This time the desire for heat surpasses everything else and I follow them inside. I can't even tell if we've been there already. Despite my sobriety, the interiors have started blending together. Perhaps my mind is freezing now.

The girls hurry through the crowd of people congregating by the kitchen area and the couches. Some partyers nurse their beers while others down the malty liquid as though it's the last one they'll ever have. When I look back to find Melissa, she's gone. Rebecca and I squeeze our way through to the other end of the living room and find an open door on the right. The other girls in our group are inside, waiting. I walk in and realize it's a bedroom. The sheets are scattered all over the place, as well as mismatched socks and an array of red solo cups and dark glass bottles with labels I don't recognize.

I feel warm; I feel safe. Melissa is in the bathroom on the other side of the room. I notice I'm still hugging myself, and I let my arms drop.

"Um, excuse me?"

We whirl around to find a guy standing in the

doorway. He steps inside and I see he's holding a key in his hand.

"This isn't a public restroom," he said. "This is my room."

Our eyes meet, and I know all he sees is a young girl who doesn't know what the hell she's doing. But I want to tell him that I understand. I want him to know that I realize the importance of your own space, your own warmth. He doesn't see it in my eyes. All he sees is my failure of a makeshift costume: the denim skirt, my plaid shirt, and no trace of a jacket or leggings whatsoever.

* * *

My senior year of high school, our English teacher asked our parents to write us a letter. There wasn't much direction with the prompt—only to speak their minds and give us insight as we looked forward to college.

"To my wonderful daughter," my mother wrote. "Here is the advice I would like to offer you as you begin the next stage of your life…. A very bright girl

I know has her own saying, 'Things happen for a reason.' Once you figure out how to handle each little situation life hands you, you usually figure out the reason it happened to begin with. And you grow a little more."

I grew out of being four, five, six years old. I broke into the later single digits, the times when you looked forward to being older. The gate disappeared from my door at night. My parents added to my room a fancy table with a glass covering on top, as well as a long blue tablecloth that glided to the floor. It added some class to the look of my space. It meant my parents trusted me with something fragile.

But the moment when my mother would write that letter was still years away. When I was around eight or nine, my brother Caleb was helping my mother with something in the basement. My days of climbing had long been over. I was wandering around the first floor and heard them below. Curious, I sat at the top step for a few minutes before a funny idea entered my mind. I stood up and slammed the basement door shut. I was just tall enough to lock it, hearing the satisfying *click* as the bolt latched inside the doorframe.

I ran upstairs to my room, just able to hear my mother's footsteps as she raced upstairs to the door she had no way of getting through. I surveyed my space quickly, locking in on the table with the glass on top. I tossed the long blue tablecloth aside and hid underneath it like it was my asylum. I giggled and held my hands over my mouth. It seemed like only a few minutes had passed—but it may have been longer—when the tablecloth was whipped aside and I was staring into my mother's angry face.

* * *

I can't bring myself to drink anything tonight. I can't keep barging in on people's homes, as much as they seemingly welcome it. It doesn't make sense to me. I don't understand how someone can welcome the feeling of being violated. To me, a house is your own space, your zone that only belongs to you.

"I want to go home," I say to Rebecca.

She nods. I'm not sure which "home" I'm talking about.

* * *

My mother had hoisted Caleb out of the high-up basement window so that he could go around the front of the house and unlock the door. Sometimes I wonder how long it would have taken me otherwise to unlock it.

But I never did time for these types of actions. They don't arrest you for stealing toys from kindergarten and telling your parents that you were told you should take them. Even when you put them back at your mother's request, but neglected to tell your teacher you stole them in the first place, nothing really happened. Yet, I understood what my mother knew little misdemeanors like these could lead up to, later in life.

When I went off to college, my mother told me to expect that there would be rough spots. She said it was impossible to find perfection anywhere. She instructed me to picture myself riding a wave in the ocean. It would lift me up and it would let me down —and maybe turn me over in the sand a couple of times.

"But," she wrote on in her letter, "I do not know of any person more up for the challenge than you. You are so completely independent. You have always been mature beyond your years, and this year you have blossomed beyond what I would ever have imagined you could."

I don't climb the gates anymore; I don't take pride in locking people out or forcing myself in. I'm leaving the block party, with Rebecca by my side. I notice how she doesn't stumble—rather, she walks in step with me. Our group follows close behind.

I don't think I could gauge how much I've actually grown, had my mother never been there to call me on it. I don't think I would have remembered how cunning I really was, how intelligent I can be now, had she not told me years later that she knew I used to climb the gate—or had she not recalled the day when she asked my kindergarten teacher if I returned the toys I took, only to be given a confused, puzzled expression in return.

"If," she quotes her favorite poem by Rudyard Kipling in her letter, "you can trust yourself when all men doubt you / But make allowance for their doubting too. / If you can wait and not be tired by waiting. / Or being lied about—don't deal in lies. / Or being hated, don't give way to hating. / And yet, don't look too good or talk too wise."

I know I don't look too good in a makeshift cowgirl costume. I wasn't too wise by agreeing to come out with my friends either. But now I've seen something new, something perceived as normal in this college culture. Maybe I'll get used to it. Maybe it'll help me grow in some way that I wouldn't have suspected before. These girls know my limits for now.

Or perhaps the existence of limits has been the culprit all along. That being said, I still don't think I'll wear a jacket next year.

About the Author

J.S. Rosen is a native of St. Louis who now calls the southern United States home. When she's not writing, she can be found baking, hiking, and spending time with her husband and their dog.

CPSIA information can be obtained
at www.ICGtesting.com
Printed in the USA
JSHW011209120323
38764JS00003B/118